FUN WITH FIRST-GRADE FRIENDS

The Lunch Box Surprise

and

Recess Mess

Grace Maccarone

Illustrated by Betsy Lewin

Cartwheel BOOKS®

SCHOLASTIC INC.

New York   Toronto   London   Auckland   Sydney
Mexico City   New Delhi   Hong Kong   Buenos Aires

Cover illustration copyright © 1996 by Betsy Lewin.

The Lunch Box Surprise (ISBN 0-590-26267-X)
Text copyright © 1995 by Grace Maccarone.
Illustrations copyright © 1995 by Betsy Lewin.

Recess Mess (ISBN 0-590-73878-X)
Text copyright © 1996 by Grace Maccarone.
Illustrations copyright © 1996 by Betsy Lewin.

All rights reserved. Published by Scholastic Inc.
SCHOLASTIC, CARTWHEEL BOOKS, FIRST-GRADE FRIENDS, and associated logos are trademarks and/or registered trademarks of Scholastic Inc.

ISBN-13: 978-0-439-93444-2
ISBN-10: 0-439-93444-3

12 11 10 9 8 7 6 5 4 3 2 1   7 8 9 10 11 12/0

Printed in the U.S.A.   23

This collection first printing, September 2007

FUN WITH FIRST-GRADE FRIENDS

The Lunch Box Surprise

To Betsy Molisani—Thanks for the lunch!
—G.M.

To Angie "Nana" Cosentino
—B.L.

Recess Mess

To Gina Shaw,
who spells very well
—G.M.

To Samuel Gus Ziebel
and Jordan Emily Zwetchkenbaum
—B.L.

THE LUNCH BOX SURPRISE

by Grace Maccarone
Illustrated by Betsy Lewin

"It's time for lunch.
It's time to eat,"
the teacher says.
"Now take your seat!"

"My lunch is best,"
say Jan and Pam

and Kim and Dan

and Max and Sam.

Jan has peanut butter,
bread, and jam.

Pam has soup.

Dan has ham.

Kim has tuna,
toast, and cheese.

Max has chicken,
rice, and peas.

But Sam has nothing—
not a spot.
Sam has nothing!
His mom forgot!

Sam is surprised.
Sam is sad.
Sam is hungry.
Sam is mad!

But Max and Kim,
Jan, Dan, and Pam
feel sorry
for their sad friend, Sam.

Jan gives Sam
peanut butter,
bread, and jam.

Pam gives him soup.
Dan gives him ham.

Kim gives him tuna,
toast, and cheese.

Max gives him chicken,
rice, and peas.

Now Sam is not sad
and Sam is not mad.
This is the best lunch
Sam ever had!

RECESS MESS

by **Grace Maccarone**

Illustrated by **Betsy Lewin**

Sam, Dan, Pam,
Kim, Max, and Jan
put away books
as fast as they can.

They put on coats.

They get in line.

They go outside.
It's recess time.

Dan runs.

Pam rolls.

Max slides.

Kim crawls.

Jan climbs.

Sam swings.

Sam swings.

Sam falls.

Dan throws. Pam catches.

Jan dances. Max hops.

Kim skips.

Sam jumps.

Sam jumps. Sam stops.

Sam looks for the boys' room.
He needs to go.
He sees two doors.
But wait! Oh, no!
Sam never used
this room before.
Sam tries to read
what's on the door.

B-O-Y?
G-I-R-L?
But Sam can't read.
And Sam can't spell.

What should Sam do?
Which should Sam use?
Sam gets an idea
to help him choose.

Sam will wait
and wait some more
for a boy or a girl
to come out of the door.